More TWO-MINUTE MINUTE MYSTERIES

Donald J. Sobol

AN
APPLE®
PAPERBACK

SCHOLASTIC INC.
New York Toronto London Auckland Sydney

For Kurt Severin

Other books by the author
available from Scholastic Inc.:

Two-Minute Mysteries
Still More Two-Minute Mysteries
Encyclopedia Brown Carries On
Encyclopedia Brown and the Case
    of the Dead Eagles
Encyclopedia Brown Sets the Pace
Encyclopedia Brown and the Case
    of the Exploding Plumbing
Encyclopedia Brown Solves Them All

ISBN 0-590-40129-7

12 11 10 9 8 7 6 5 4 3   6 7 8 9/8 0 1/9

Printed in the U.S.A.   06

The Case of the
AIRPORT
KILLING

"At 8 A.M. on Monday, March 4, 1968, you were drinking coffee in a rear booth in the Sandwich Shop at the airport?" asked the district attorney.

"I was," answered McCarthy, the murder defendant.

"And you didn't see the man in the booth across the aisle — not five feet from you — stabbed to death!"

"No, I was reading the local morning newspaper."

"The cashier remembers you. You were in an awful hurry. You gave her a half-dollar in payment of a 15-cent check, and you didn't wait for your change."

"I had to catch a plane."

"You were aware of the time, but you didn't notice the man in the next booth was dead — with a knife sticking out of his chest?"

"I might have seen him, but I never looked directly at him."

"You didn't hear him order eggs and coffee?"

"I might have. I don't remember. I was busy reading the New York Stock Exchange listings. I own some shares."

"How long did that take you?"

"A couple of minutes. Then I read the market news. There was a long article forecasting steel prospects for next year. After I finished reading the article, I noticed the time. I had less than two minutes to catch my plane to Los Angeles."

In the rear of the courtroom, Dr. Haledjian leaned over and whispered to Inspector Winters: "If he isn't convicted of murder, he'll draw a stiff sentence for perjury!"

How come?

The defendant claimed he was so busy checking stocks in the morning newspaper that he didn't notice the killing. Impossible! On Monday, local morning newspapers do not carry stock exchange transactions.

The Case of the
ANXIOUS
NEPHEW

"I'm worried about my Uncle Phil," Stephen Bates' voice was anxious over the telephone. "He failed to keep a dinner engagement with me tonight. Do you mind meeting me at his place — say in half an hour?"

Dr. Haledjian agreed and he was waiting in the lobby of Philip Bates' apartment building when Stephen arrived by cab.

"My uncle thought he was being followed the last couple of days," said Stephen. "He keeps a great deal of cash in a wall safe in his den. Unfortunately, he isn't exactly secretive about it."

"Did you try to reach him tonight?" asked Haledjian.

"When he didn't show up for dinner, I telephoned his home. I got no answer."

Leaving the elevator on the fourteenth floor, the two men walked rapidly to the door of Philip Bates' bachelor apartment. It was unlocked. In the entrance hall burned the only light.

"Better have a look in the den," suggested Haledjian.

Stephen nodded and led the way. He paused at the door to the darkened room. "There's a floor lamp in the corner," he said, and disappeared into the darkness. An instant later the room was bathed in light. Directly behind the desk a small oval safe door was open. Stephen stood in a corner, one hand on the lamp, an expression of alarm twisting his face. He stepped back over the unmoving form of his uncle, who lay at his feet. "I-is he dead?"

Haledjian knelt beside Philip Bates. "No, a nasty blow on the head, but not fatal — lucky for you! You went to a lot of trouble to throw me off the scent. Then at the last minute you practically confessed to the crime!"

What was Stephen's mistake?

In leaving the floor lamp, Stephen had "stepped back over" his uncle. Thus, in going to the lamp, he'd had to step over his uncle, which he did. But only a man who knew beforehand that Philip Bates lay on the floor could have avoided tripping over him in the darkness.

The Case of the
ARCTIC HERO

"Don't tell me," said Dr. Haledjian. "Let me guess. You made a play for a young lady, but got your lines fouled and your face slapped."

Cyril Makin, the luckless Lothario, nodded glumly. "This time I was absolutely sure I had my story down pat. Yet something went wrong. I can't figure what.

"You've heard of Gertrude Morgan?" he asked. "Her grandfather sailed with Admiral Byrd and a cousin climbed Mt. Everest with the Eggler party. If you haven't combed icicles from your whiskers you don't rate with her.

"I took her to dinner Christmas Eve, and it seemed a good time to trundle out my Arctic Circle yarn," continued the youth. "I opened by commenting that I had once spent Christmas Eve in less comfortable surroundings.

"Then I told her about the morning Lt. Craven and I were mushing back to the Navy's Arctic Observation Weather Station. Suddenly

Craven fell and fractured his leg. Ten minutes later the stretch of ice we were crossing broke loose. We began to drift out to sea.

"I realized Craven and I and the dogs would freeze to death unless I started a fire. Alas, we had used up all of our matches. I got out a small magnifying glass from our instrument kit and, tearing off sheets from our reports, laid them on a steel instrument box. By focusing the sun's rays through the glass onto the paper, I started a hearty blaze.

"Fortunately, a cutter picked us up after 24 hours. The captain said I was a bit of a hero."

"But not Miss Morgan," said Haledjian. "And no wonder!"

What was wrong with Cyril's story?

In the Arctic Circle on Christmas Eve Cyril could not have started a fire by using the sun's rays.

As every schoolboy knows (or should), the sun disappears in the far north from October to about March.

8

The Case of the
BOOK
CONTRACT

"I should like a moment to scan the contract," said the scholarly, white-haired man who called himself Everett Willy. "If there is a major point of disagreement, I should prefer to know it now."

"Of course," agreed Morgan, the publisher. As Dr. Haledjian watched from the leather office couch, the publisher passed a contract of three sheets across his desk to Willy.

Haledjian observed Willy's eyes skim the lines of small type. The pages of the contract were flipped rapidly.

"It appears to be satisfactory," said Willy, putting the contract into his attaché case. "I shall have to read it carefully when I am home, you understand. Tomorrow you will have my answer."

Smiling, Willy rose, shook hands, and departed.

"All right," Haledjian said to Morgan. "Why did you ask me to sit in on a book contract discussion?"

"Twenty years ago," replied Morgan, "Everett Willy wrote a masterpiece on the English language; it's become the standard text on the subject. No one ever saw him, however. He was a man of mystery.

"For the past ten years there have been rumors that he was in South America working on a new book, better than the first. A month ago came rumors that the new book was done, but that Willy had died a few days after completing it. The man who presented himself to me just now has the manuscript — and it's superb! But is the man really Everett Willy? Or is he an imposter trying to profit from another man's manuscript?"

"An imposter!" answered Haledjian without hesitation.

What made Haledjian so sure?

The real Everett Willy, a master of the English language, would not have committed one of the most common errors in the language — misusing the word "scan."

The verb "to scan" means to examine intensively. The imposter, like most semieducated persons, thought it means "to skim" in reading.

The Case of the
BOTTLE OF CYANIDE

Arthur Maxim sagged in an easy chair. His right hand lay on his lap, clutched about a bottle of cyanide.

"He's been dead about fifteen minutes," Dr. Haledjian told Carter. "Have you called the police?"

"Yes — but I called you first. I knew you were at the hotel. Arthur was depressed, but — good heavens! — I never dreamed he'd kill himself!"

"You knew him well?" asked Haledjian.

"We were kids together," replied Carter. "Since his wife divorced him, he's been despondent. I suggested this vacation. He seemed better yesterday. We played golf and fished.

"Half an hour ago I went down to the lobby for a newspaper. Just as I returned, he drank that bottle in his hand."

Inspector Winters arrived. Haledjian summed up his findings.

"You'll notice how lax the body is," said the

11

sleuth, pointing to the drooping position the corpse had assumed in the chair. "Cyanide kills instantly, and the muscles go limp.

"Maxim appears to have committed suicide by drinking cyanide. But no conclusion is possible till we know for certain the cause of death."

Two days later the inspector told Haledjian: "The lab confirms that Maxim's death was due to cyanide."

"That clinches it!" was the reply. "Arrest Carter on suspicion of murder!"

Why?

As cyanide "kills instantly, and the muscles go limp," Maxim couldn't possibly have held the bottle clutched in his hand. It had to have been put there after death!

The Case of the
BULLET IN
THE BACK

Dr. Haledjian and the tour's other saddle-sore dudes gazed down upon two rotting pieces of timber.

"Now this here spot," intoned their unshaven little guide, "is called Bushwack Alley, bein' so known for the shootin' of two deputies back in '73.

"Elbow Bend was a thrivin' town in them days, and Doc Pressman's house stood right here. One night there's some gunplay in back, and a stranger staggers into Doc's kitchen.

"The doc removes a .44 slug from the stranger's upper back, loans him a clean shirt, and fixes his right arm in a sling.

"Says the stranger: 'I was crossin' South Street when I heerd gun-fightin' and seen a fella runnin' from two lawmen. I joined the chase. The fella ambushed us in the deadend behind your house, Doc, killed the lawmen, and wounded me.'

"Just then Sheriff Pell and Clyde Everest, the local undertaker, storm in.

13

" 'I bet that's him!' cries Everest.

"The sheriff draws his gun. 'A gunslinger robbed the freight office and killed two of my best deputies, mister. Don't give me no trouble.'

" 'Hold on!' shouts the stranger. 'I was helpin' your deputies chase the real thief!'

" 'The bullet in your back says you was doin' the runnin', not the chasin',' " points out Everest.

"Seein' as there was no witnesses," concluded the guide, "the sheriff just naturally had to string up the stranger."

"Naturally," sighed Haledjian. "Whoever heard of a western sheriff hanging the guilty man!"

What was the basis for Haledjian's remark?

As there were no witnesses, Everest could not know the stranger had been shot in the back, unless Everest himself did the shooting. The stranger was wearing the doc's clean shirt when Everest, the real thief, saw him in the house.

The Case of the
CONFEDERATE
HALF-DOLLAR

Driving through a dilapidated neighborhood at midnight, Dr. Haledjian abruptly stomped on his brakes. His headlights had illuminated a man lying on the sidewalk.

The man still breathed, though strangulation marks on his neck indicated the sleuth's sudden arrival had scared off the assailant in the nick of time.

The street was deserted till an elderly man stepped from the door of a decaying building nearby.

"Why, it's old Keyes! I knew this would happen. I warned him!"

"Warned him about what?" demanded Haledjian.

"About going around jingling his Confederate half-dollar. I'm Stevens. Keyes and I have lived across the hall from each other for twenty years. Ten minutes ago I heard him go out — he jingles that half-dollar all the time, as if inviting somebody to rob him."

"Is the half dollar valuable?"

"It is one of four made in 1861, and it's worth about $5,000," said Stevens. "Keyes kept it as a good luck charm. I've told him to be careful. Is it stolen?"

Haledjian refused to permit a search on the sidewalk. At the hospital, however, the coin was found in Keyes' right trouser pocket.

Haledjian telephoned Inspector Winters.

"The only other items Keyes carried were two handkerchiefs and a leather wallet containing a dollar bill," said the sleuth. "I suggest you arrest Stevens at once!"

How come?

Haledjian realized that Stevens, attempting to establish an alibi, claimed he had been in his room and that he knew Keyes had departed because he jingled his rare half-dollar.

Unfortunately for Stevens, Keyes carried nothing else in his pocket against which the rare coin could strike — and so jingle!

The Case of the
DEPARTMENT STORE MURDER

Dr. Haledjian was walking past the lingerie counters on the ground floor of a crowded department store when he was nearly gored by a bull.

"Sorry," apologized the slim young man in shirtsleeves. He bowed and proceeded on his way, agilely steering a papier-mâché bull's head through the mobs of shoppers.

Behind him trailed two hefty girls ladened with the bull's hind quarters. They were followed by a procession of slender men: two brunets bearing matador costumes, a redhead carrying several black petticoats, and four blonds each lugging a bare manikin upside down.

Haledjian observed the parade of window dressers file into a roped-off area by the back of a display window. He thought nothing of them until an hour later, when he saw a crowd and several policemen collected by the window.

"Somebody murdered Joe Johnson, a store

executive, as he sat at his desk," said Inspector Winters. "The only possible angle of fire leads back to this display window.

"The killer," added the inspector, "undoubtedly used a silencer. But what baffles me is why nobody saw him pull the gun."

"Perhaps I can help," said Haledjian, stepping outside to study the newly decorated window, which was designed to sell toreador pants at $39.98.

The four manikins, attired as matadors, stood around the papier-mâché bull. The background consisted of a screen painted to resemble a stadium filled with spectators.

"I believe I can recall the face of the murderer," Haledjian told the inspector. "Shall we go to your office and look through the albums?"

Whom did Haledjian suspect?

The redheaded man, who had apparently scooped up some petticoats from a counter and fallen in with the window dressers. As the petticoats had no place in the window, since toreador pants were shown, their only purpose was to conceal the gun!

The Case of the
DOUBLE
BLOWOUT

Dr. Haledjian was returning late at night from a hunting trip when the headlights of his car shone upon a sedan parked across the country road.

He swerved onto the shoulder to avoid a collision and braked as two of his tires blew. Suddenly four masked men appeared. They relieved him of his money and sped off in the sedan.

"A neat little caper," muttered the sleuth, playing his flashlight over the scattering of razor sharp studs that had caused the two flats.

Tramping to a farmhouse he told the farmer who answered his knocking, "I was just robbed about a mile down the road. I'll need a new tire. Can you get someone to help me?"

"Come in," the farmer invited. "I'll telephone Titusburg. Make yourself comfortable."

The farmer disappeared into the kitchen. Haledjian heard him speak over the telephone to the sheriff and then to a service station.

"The sheriff and a new tire are on the way here," the farmer said, emerging from the kitchen.

An hour later the sleuth was recounting the details of the holdup to the sheriff while a serviceman put on his spare tire and the new tire which the farmer had requested.

Then, upon Haledjian's recommendation, the sheriff arrested the farmer for being involved in the holdup.

Why?

Unless he had seen Haledjian's car, parked at night a mile from his house, the farmer could not have known what size tire to order.

The Case of the
DYING
BRAZILIAN

It had been months since Nick the Nose had slipped into Inspector Winter's office to peddle a phony tip.

"I got something on the Nilo Bernardes case," the greasy little informer confided slyly.

"Nilo Bernardes," the inspector explained to Haledjian, "is a 10-year-old boy who was kidnapped last month in Santos, Brazil. His father, a millionaire, paid the ransom. The boy has not been returned."

"Last night," said Nick, "this old guy in Pedro's Flop started to talk as he lay dying. At first he ran on about how he had lived all his life in Brazil and never did anything wrong till last month. Then he got interesting.

"He said he had sinned by collecting the ransom money for young Nilo. Before he got paid his share, he had overheard the rest of the kidnap gang plotting to kill him.

"So that night he stowed away on a freighter

and jumped ship in America. With his dying breath, he named the town in Brazil where the kidnappers are laying low.

"Of course, he spoke in Spanish and I didn't understand him. But Pedro, who is Mexican, understood and did the interpreting. Pedro will back me up.

"I figure," concluded Nick, "that the name of the town where the kidnappers are hiding is worth a bundle!"

The inspector rose, growling. Haledjian barely had time to open the office door before Nick went sailing out.

Why was Nick given the heave-ho?

Nick the Nose had bribed Pedro, the flophouse proprietor, to confirm his phony tip. However, a dying man who had "lived all his life in Brazil" wouldn't speak his last words in Spanish, but in Portuguese, the language of Brazil!

The Case of the
ESCOBI
SAPPHIRE

"The coroner just finished a preliminary examination," said Inspector Winters. "Professor Merton died of a heart attack about 11 P.M. I telephoned you because of a complication over the Escobi Sapphire."

"The ring given him by the Maharani of Isha during his trip to the East last year," recalled Haledjian.

"And worth an emperor's ransom," added the inspector. "Miss Samuels, Professor Merton's long-time secretary, claims he presented it to her last week. She kept it hidden in her room and told no one — afraid of causing family resentment. However, Anita Merton, a teenage niece, insists she saw her uncle wearing the sapphire an hour before he died."

"Thus the question is whether Miss Samuels received the sapphire as a gift, or by stripping it from a dead man's hand," said Haledjian, as he examined the body.

Edwin Merton, lecturer in Rabbinic Hebrew, lay slumped in a heavy leather armchair. A red volume, open to reveal Hebrew print, lay where it had fallen at the moment of death.

Haledjian asked to see the niece, who told her story with cool assurance.

"I was in the den with Uncle between nine and ten o'clock," she said. "I had some typing to do, and he said I might go ahead, as he was merely reading for pleasure."

"From the red book by the chair?"

"Yes."

"And was he wearing the Escobi Sapphire?"

"He was. I sat here at the desk, not eight feet from him. I couldn't have been mistaken. Occasionally, when his right hand turned the page, the jewel, which he wore on his little finger, flashed brilliantly."

Haledjian's face tightened in a rare display of anger. "You are a jealous young lady. I suggest you go directly to Miss Samuels and apologize for maliciously attempting to discredit her."

Why?

The professor was reading a book written in Hebrew, which is read from "back to front." He therefore would not have turned the pages with his right hand, but with his left.

The Case of the
FASHION
CAMERAMAN

"I was taking fashion movies this morning when the men who held up the American Bank ran smack in front of the camera," Ed Courtney said over the telephone.

"Somebody broke into my studio this afternoon," he continued. "I'm sure it was the bank robbers. Luckily, the film was in the developer and they missed it. Can you come over? I may need help."

Dr. Haledjian assured the frightened man he was on his way. When he arrived, a movie projector was humming. The criminologist had a fleeting glimpse of a fashion model on the screen a split second before the film ran out with a snapping clack.

"I've got close-ups of the robbers near the start," said Courtney, flipping off the machine. Quickly he removed the reel and dropped it into a black bag.

"I'm off to the police with this," he said.

"Would you mind staying here, just in case those cutthroats are watching, while I sneak out the back?"

Haledjian agreed. "But be careful," he warned.

"Courtney wasn't careful enough," Sheriff Monohan told Haledjian three days later. "He drove off the road. His body was discovered in his wrecked convertible at the bottom of Gurnsey Ravine an hour ago, along with this."

The sheriff held up the reel of film. "Let's have a look at it," he said, threading a projector.

Courtney's pictures were professionally perfect — except they were entirely of skinny fashion models in bizarre clothes.

"There's the proof that Courtney was murdered," said Haledjian. "The bank robbers edited out the hold-up sequences and then tried to make his death look like an auto accident!"

What was Haledjian's proof?

Courtney had removed the film from his projector without rewinding it. Hence, unless it had been tampered with, the models would have been walking upside down and backwards when shown in the sheriff's office.

The Case of the
FAST
TRAVELER

"Try the manual dial," suggested Dr. Haledjian, after Captain Gordon of the Miami police had punched all the push-buttons of the radio and had got only static.

Immediately, music poured out noisily.

"Do you always play the radio so loud?" snapped Gordon at the pale youth riding handcuffed in the reat seat of the car.

"I play it any way I feel like. It's my convertible," retorted McGuire.

Haledjian turned down the volume. For the rest of the drive to headquarters he thoughtfully reviewed the case.

The Chicago National Bank had been held up four days ago, and more than half a million dollars was stolen. One of the holdup men, according to the Chicago Police Department's informer, was Billy McGuire, a young ex-convict. The informer said McGuire had headed straight for Miami in a green convertible after the crime.

27

That morning the convertible had been spotted in the driveway of a big-time Florida gambler. The gambler swore the youth had been living with him in Miami for two months, and therefore couldn't have taken part in a Chicago robbery.

A search of the gambler's home disclosed McGuire's summer clothing in the guest room, and throughout the house a typical amount of underworld luxury, including a connoisseur's collection of popular records. But none of the stolen money.

"You're wastin' your time, Gordon," taunted McGuire. "Hey — tune up the radio. That's the Dixie Bobcats. Ain't they the greatest?"

"Like popular music, do you?" inquired Haledjian.

"I like a lot of things. Especially this Florida climate," sneered McGuire.

"Enjoy it while you can," answered Haledjian, "once this car is back in Chicago, you and your gambler friend will have to think up a new alibi."

Why?

Two reasons: McGuire's lack of a suntan, and the fact that the push-buttons of the car radio had not yet been adjusted to the Florida stations. They were still tuned to Chicago frequencies, as investigation later showed.

The Case of the
FATAL SLIP

Dr. Haledjian parked his car and offered his services to the state trooper. The policeman was about to question one of the drivers involved in a tragic accident on the winding mountain road.

The driver was young, broad-shouldered, and dressed in evening attire that was spotless, except at the trouser cuffs and shoes. These were splattered with mud.

Dazedly he told his story.

"I was taking Joan to the dance. That other car crossed the centerline, forcing me wide. The road is slippery from the rain this morning, and I skidded off the embankment.

"Luckily," he continued, "I escaped injury when my car hit that tree. But Joan was knocked unconscious. I carried her back toward the road. As I passed the side of the ravine, I slipped and she tumbled from my arms. It — it was horrible!"

"I didn't cross the line," insisted the other

driver. When I heard his car crash through the rail, I braked and hurried back to help."

"What did you see?" asked Haledjian.

"He was carrying the young lady," admitted the second driver. "As he got near the embankment, he slipped to his knees and the girl fell without a sound."

Haledjian descended the treacherously wet embankment. The intermingling of grass, rocks, and mud made a search for footprints useless.

At the spot where the first driver said he lost his hold, Haledjian could see the broken figure of the girl a hundred feet below.

Back on the road he said, "I should hold both these men on suspicion of murder, officer."

Why?

Haledjian suspected that the two men had staged the accident. When the driverless car missed the ravine and crashed into the tree instead, they had thrown the girl to her death. Had the young man "slipped to his knees" in the mud, as his overeager accomplice claimed, his clothes in that area would not have been "spotless."

The Case of the
HEALTH FORMULA

Bertie Tilford, the Englishman who had sold the Brooklyn Bridge more often than any man alive, ushered a robust young man into Dr. Haledjian's living room.

"Meet Howard Kent, the physical wonder of the century!" exclaimed Bertie.

Kent dropped to the floor and commenced doing pushups like a trip-hammer. Then he jumped to his feet and began to remove his clothing.

Haledjian barely had time to note that his suit, though it fit well and was neatly pressed, was threadbare. His left shoe had a large hole in the sole.

Stripped, Kent flexed his massive physique in all directions.

"Would you believe that he gained 70 pounds of solid muscle in the past seven months?" asked Bertie. "He's developed a secret, high-protein food formula, which, combined with proper exercise — "

"And you need capital to market the formula," said Haledjian.

"Quite so," sighed Bertie. "Why the suit Kent's wearing is two years old. He's put every cent into perfecting his secret formula. And I am, frankly, temporarily out of funds, or I should plunge for the whole thing myself.

"All we need is $15,000, dear boy," Bertie ran on. "You'll better mankind and realize a fortune besides!"

"Not today," muttered Haledjian darkly. "You'd have a better chance of selling me the Brooklyn Bridge!"

What was wrong with Bertie's pitch?

Kent's suit, which Bertie claimed was "two years old," still "fit well," though he had supposedly put on 70 pounds "in the past seven months." Impossible!

The Case of the
HORSESHOE PITCHER

On the day the Carson home was burglarized, the family was away. They had, however, allowed the neighborhood children to play in their large backyard.

The yard was well equipped for children, and encircled by a seven-foot stone wall into which admission was gained by a solid oak door.

Dr. Haledjian entered the yard to call Billy Wills home for supper. Billy and three other boys were pitching horseshoes.

Without arguing, Billy stopped playing. He picked up his baseball glove and accompanied Haledjian home.

"I gotta obey," the boy said. "Tomorrow is my birthday."

At Billy's house, Haledjian saw Mrs. Wills talking with Ed Tate, a neighbor and an ex-convict.

"The game would have been over in a couple more innings," Billy said disappointedly. "Gosh,

33

if I had the right equipment, we could have played here and finished before dinner."

Ed Tate grinned. "Maybe you'll get it for your birthday."

To Billy's mother, Tate said, "Thanks for the loan of the wrenches. I've been fighting the washing machine all day."

The next morning Haledjian read that the Carson home had been robbed. Upon learning that Ed Tate had given Billy Wills a horseshoe pitching set for his birthday, the sleuth advised the police to pick up Tate for questioning.

How come?

Tate's remark about working "all day" was an obvious alibi. As Billy Wills carried a baseball glove and used the word "innings," Tate should have assumed he wanted baseball equipment for his birthday.

Only by being inside the Carson house could Tate have seen Billy pitching horseshoes — a game in which the term "inning" is also used.

The Case of the
HOT TIP

Before Inspector Winters could bellow a protest, Nick the Nose had slipped into his office.

"I got something this time," the little informer insisted. "Last night I'm sleeping in this abandoned warehouse when I hear noises. A voice says, 'Did you glim that piece on page 29 about Mrs. Vandermill?'

"There's a hole in the floor," continued Nick. "I can see four tough eggs sitting in the room below. One of them picks up a newspaper and turns to the back page and starts reading out loud. What he reads goes something like this: 'The Baritoni collection of jewels has been purchased by Mrs. C. Worthington Vandermill of 292 Sea Cliff Heights. Mrs. Vandermill told reporters she will keep the jewels, valued at more than a million dollars, in her house, which she claims is burglar proof.'

"The four guys begin to laugh," Nick went on. "One guy says, 'Harry, make sure the car is running good, because tomorrow night we're going to pay Mrs. Vandermill a quiet little visit.' "

"There is no Sea Cliff Heights in this city," said Inspector Winters. He lifted a hand.

Nick the Nose remained unshaken. "They were probably reading an out-of-town paper. They'll be back tonight. For ten bucks I'll take you — "

The inspector rose menacingly.

"Five?" yelped Nick.

"Five — fingers," growled the inspector, putting five on Nick's collar and five on the seat of his pants. Haledjian opened the door wide as the little informer flew out into the hall.

Why wasn't Nick paid off?

Although the article on Mrs. Vandermill appeared on page 29, it was read from the "back page."

Alas for Nick the Nose, the back page of a newspaper always has an even number.

The Case of the
JADE MONKEY

"The Staffords were known to be in reduced circumstances. Owed everybody," said Henderson, the insurance investigator. "The ten thousand dollars they'll collect on the shattered art treasure will save their scalps."

"Then it's your conviction the jade monkey was deliberately broken?" asked Dr. Haledjian.

"Of course, but I can't budge the eyewitness, Mrs. Endicott. She's the Staffords' neighbor and closest friend.

"A few moments before the alleged 'accident,' Mrs. Endicott received a box containing a mink coat. It was her first fur, and since it was a warm August day, she went directly upstairs to unpack and hang it in the storage closet.

"The window next to the storage closet," continued the insurance man, "is the only one in her house which has a view into the Staffords' bedroom. After hanging the coat, Mrs. Endicott heard Mrs. Stafford scream and saw her neighbor

37

stumble into the jade monkey. It sailed through the open bedroom window and shattered on the patio below.

"The fur company's driver noted the Endicott delivery was made at 3:30 P.M. About a minute later, he heard Mrs. Stafford scream. Rushing from the truck, he saw the fragments of the jade monkey, and both women at their windows."

"As it was a warm August day," interrupted Haledjian, "why wasn't there a screen on the Stafford window?"

"It was being repaired. That was the first angle I investigated. About the only thing I've got to go on is the hunch Mrs. Endicott is lying for her friend."

"I should take the matter to court before paying," agreed Haledjian. "And make sure you have several women on the jury."

What did Haledjian mean by the last remark?

Mrs. Endicott's presence at the *only* window where she could substantiate Mrs. Stafford's claim was obviously part of a plot to collect the insurance money. Haledjian realized other women would instantly see through it.

No woman receiving her first mink would ever put it directly into storage. She would try it on and purr over it.

The Case of the
LADY
LARRUPER

The cab driver sported a shiner three shades of blue, a swollen lip, and a mouthful of missing teeth.

"We found your cab abandoned by Pier 9," said Inspector Winters. "You didn't report it missing, and you weren't at work today. Come on, now. What happened?"

The cabbie, a sizeable young man, looked at the floor. Finally, under the prodding of Inspector Winters and Dr. Haledjian, he shamefacedly detailed the manner of his wounds.

"I picked up this fare on the corner of Madison and 49th," he said. "She was a real big doll with a husky voice. She yanked open the door and gave me an address in the west Bronx, and then climbed in.

"When we reached Riverdale, I swung off the parkway, and she suddenly told me to pull up. It was dark and the street was one of those private roads with no through traffic.

" 'All right, baby,' she said. 'Play it smart and

you won't get hurt.'

"I slid from behind the wheel and opened the door for her. 'Lady,' I said. 'You shouldn't play like a tough guy. Out!'

"She got out sort of funny. 'Want it the hard way, do you?' she said.

"Pow! She rammed me in the eye with a fist. I went down, surprised. She was big, but not that big.

"She belted me twice more, fast, like a pro, once in the mouth and once in the stomach. When I woke up, my wallet was gone, and so were four teeth and my cab. I was too sick to work today. Holy cats, I never thought a dame could strong-arm me to sleep."

"We have your cab," said Haledjian. "And if we can't recover your wallet, it might comfort you to know that it was undoubtedly a man dressed as a woman who beat you up."

How did Haledjian know?

The "big doll" gave the address, and *then* climbed into the cab.

Haledjian knew what the cabbie should have known: that 90 per cent of men riders tell the address before sitting down — while outside the cab, or on the way. And 99 per cent of the women passengers never give their destination until *after* they are settled on the seat.

If you're a doubter, ask any big city cabbie.

The Case of the
LINCOLN
LETTER

"It might be genuine," murmured Dr. Fry, chief of the crime lab.

Inspector Winters peered through a magnifying glass at the ragged sheet of foolscap. He read the writing, from which part had been torn:

"'. . . in Gettysburg at the Wills home facing the public square. Bands blared, serenading whomever spoke. I begged to be excused. The crowd was little pleased. The band played the national anthem and moved on to Seward's. . . .'"

The last sentence ran into a tear. However, the signature was unmarred — "A. Lincoln."

"It might be worth tens of thousands of dollars," said Dr. Fry.

"For an incomplete letter of President Lincoln's?" inquired the inspector. "Are they that rare?"

"Look at the reverse side," advised Dr. Fry.

The inspector released a low whistle of astonishment. On the other side of the sheet was scrawled a partial draft of the Gettysburg address!

"I found it by accident in the old Bible my sister keeps in the attic," said Sy "The Weasel" McCloskey.

"Wasn't that where you found the counterfeit tens last year?" put in the inspector sarcastically.

Dr. Fry interrupted. "I'll run some chemical tests on the paper. It'll take a couple of days."

"The paper turned out to be the right age," a surprised Inspector Winters reported to Dr. Haledjian. "I'll wager you'll never guess the value of that one little sheet!"

"About 10 cents — to a police museum," replied Haledjian. "It is obviously a forgery."

What was the weasel's error?

The two words, "national anthem."
While *The Star Spangled Banner* was the foremost patriotic song of Lincoln's day, it did not officially become our national anthem until 1931. During his presidency there was no national anthem.

The Case of the
LOCKED
WINE CELLAR

Because Wentworth Boyd invariably caught the 9:53 express Friday morning and arrived at his country home exactly two hours later, Dr. Haledjian was able to solve the theft of $50,000 from Boyd's wall safe.

One Friday Boyd broke his habit without advising anyone. On this day he arrived home shortly before midnight and found his front door ajar. Down in the basement, locked in the wine cellar, he heard his secretary, Nigel Arbuter, shouting for help.

"Coming!" cried Boyd.

"Mr. Boyd!" called Arbuter. "Robbers. I heard them say they'd catch the midnight train back to New York City!"

Boyd freed Arbuter, telephoned the police, and drove to the station. Too late. The train had already pulled out, foiling the police as well.

Dr. Haledjian, at Boyd's request, made his investigation the next day.

43

"You say two masked robbers forced you at gunpoint to unlock the safe?" he inquired.

"That's right," said Arbuter. "Then they forced a pill — some sort of sleeping potion — down my throat. I awoke in the wine cellar just before Mr. Boyd came downstairs."

Haledjian inspected the wine cellar, a windowless room 13 feet by 9 feet. The door locked from the outside. A single 40-watt bulb cast dim but adequate illumination.

Haledjian inspected the wine cellar, a win- watch. "Were you wearing it at the time of the robbery?"

"Why, y-yes," replied the secretary.

"Then kindly tell us where you hid the money you helped steal!" Haledjian ordered.

What was Arbuter's slip?

As the wine cellar was windowless, Arbuter could not, from his watch, have known how long he'd been unconscious, or whether it was near to the noon or midnight train. Indeed, since Boyd always in the past came home at noon, Arbuter, unless he'd seen Boyd arriving and had his accomplices lock him in, would have supposed it was noon — twelve hours too late to chase the robbers.

The Case of the
LOST
SPECTACLES

"How did you obtain a key to the Carlin home?" demanded Inspector Winters.

"See here," retorted Bartlett, "I've been an old friend of the Carlins for twenty years. I resent your —"

"I've just spoken with John Carlin by long distance," said the inspector evenly. "He claims there was ten thousand dollars in negotiable bonds in his strongbox. There's not ten cents there now. So begin at the beginning."

Bartlett sputtered, and then said: "Carlin asked me to check his house before he returns from Florida on Tuesday. I had intended to drop by tomorrow. I went today instead because it's been below freezing for the past week, and I thought I'd make sure there was enough heat in the house."

Bartlett gazed momentarily at the heavy icicles on the window. "Carlin had mailed a key to me from Miami. As I entered the house about nine this morning, I heard a noise in the study.

" 'Who's there?' I called, and immediately opened the study door. There were two of them. I hadn't a chance once they knocked my spectacles off. I can't see ten feet without them. The pair tied me up, and it wasn't till three hours later that I managed to work free and call the police."

"Could you identify either of the thieves?"

"If I ever saw them again," said Bartlett.

"Did you turn up the heat?"

"Why, no," answered Bartlett hesitantly. "The thermostat was set for 75, and the house was quite warm enough."

In talking to Haledjian the next day, the inspector said, "I'm convinced Bartlett broke into Carlin's strongbox, but I've nothing to hold him on."

"Nothing," asserted Haledjian, "except that he never saw two thieves in the study."

Why not?

Entering a house heated to 75 degrees from the outdoors on a below freezing day, Bartlett could not have seen anything. His glasses would have been steamed over completely.

The Case of the
LOST STAMP

Dr. Haledjian squatted in the sand in front of Murphy's oceanside home and gazed intently at a seagull's footprints that led to the ocean.

"The gull ran across the beach in a takeoff within the past half hour," said Haledjian. "Else, the high tide of half an hour ago would have obliterated its prints."

"Good grief!" said Murphy. "I asked you out here to help me calm down DeCovey when he arrives, not to tell me about seagulls."

"So you said," replied Haledjian sarcastically. "You have the only two existing one-penny Guiani of the 1857 issue. But one stamp blew into the ocean."

"Both stamps were on my desk, ready for DeCovey to examine," said Murphy. "He promised to pay $10,000 for the better one."

"You said the window behind your desk —

47

the one facing the ocean — was open?" inquired Haledjian.

"Yes, a strong wind was blowing from the land all morning. Suddenly the window on that side blow open. In the cross draft, one of the stamps blew off the desk and sailed right into the ocean. I was lucky to save the other!"

"There's not a breath of wind now."

"It stopped dead half an hour ago," said Murphy. "About the time I telephoned you to come over."

"If one of two existing Guianis is worth $10,000, the sole remaining one will be worth at least $20,000 to DeCovey," said Haledjian. "You wanted me to corroborate your story. I won't — because you still have the 'missing' other!"

What made Haledjian so sure?

The seagull's footprints proved the wind blew from ocean, not from the land. So the stamp could not have been blown into the water. A seagull, like an airplane, takes off against the wind!

The Case of the
MARATHON RUNNER

While motoring through South America, Dr. Haledjian arrived at a forest village half an hour before the start of the annual 26-mile foot race.

Although the race was held as the climax of the harvest festival, a joyous occasion, both villagers and runners seemed blanketed in gloom.

Haledjian asked the race's lone official for the reason.

"The winner," said the official, "used to receive a prize equal to $1,000. When the old landlord died, his son took over, and he entered his own son Juan in the race. Juan has won every year since. Thus the family saves the $1,000.

"Under the new landlord's rules, the runners are timed. They go off separately, one every five minutes, instead of together. Juan always starts first.

"The course goes through the forest there, a hundred yards away, and describes a circle.

The runners return up the same path to finish at the starting line.

"I am sure Juan merely runs a hundred yards into the woods, hides, and runs out at the proper time.

"I am the only official. As I come from another village, I do not fear the landlord. I would like to prove Juan cheats, but no one will help me. Here everyone is afraid to complain. If there is no race, the landlord threatened to increase taxes," concluded the official.

"You don't need any help but a tape measure," said Haledjian. "Before the race, measure —"

Measure what?

Measure Juan's calves. And measure them again at the end of the race. After covering 26 miles, a runner's calves will have increased an inch or more.

The Case of the
MILLION-TO-ONE SHOT

"The law of averages will sooner or later produce an extraordinary event," said Dr. Haledjian. "If taken by itself, such an event appears as a phenomenon — the product of wildest chance. Actually, it is but a logical variation from the common mass of nearly similar events."

Haledjian paused to hand Octavia a cup of coffee.

Then he resumed. "An excellent illustration is the disappearance of the bullets in the duel fought by the French twins, Marcel and Henri Laval, in 1857.

"Except that Marcel was left-handed, the twins were so alike that even their parents had difficulty telling them apart.

"Henri and Marcel received excellent military educations, and were soon reputed the best marksmen in the French Army. Inevitably, they fell in love with the same damsel. For young men of honor, one solution only was possible. A duel.

51

"You may picture it now, after a hundred years. The brothers standing back to back as had hundreds before them; then marching and wheeling at the count like mirror images.

"They fired simultaneously. To the seconds, the shots sounded as one. By a miracle, the brothers weren't scratched though both confessed to having aimed to kill.

"The pistols were examined and found in perfect working order. Yet neither in the barn behind Marcel, nor the fence behind Henri was either bullet located.

"The disappearance of the bullets into thin air had a mystic effect on the twins. They resigned their commissions. As the object of the duel ran off with a Hungarian nobleman, they married twin sisters of a merchant of Marseille.

"Now I've given you the clues — the law of averages and the similarity of the twins, Octavia, my dear," concluded Haledjian. "You should have no trouble in determining what really happened to the two bullets."

What?

The bullets fell on the ground between the twin brothers. They had collided and fused in midair!

The Case of the
MISSING
FINGERPRINTS

A young farmer, responding to a radio bulletin describing the stolen car used by four masked men in the holdup of the First National Bank, reported that the car had been abandoned near his farm. The four occupants had fled in such haste that they left the four doors wide open.

Shortly after Inspector Winters and Dr. Haledjian reached the scene, another patrol car arrived. Out stepped a hefty man who said, "I'm Carlson, fingerprints. Headquarters sent me. Can I start?"

The Inspector nodded, and Carlson opened his kit and began dusting the steering wheel of the getaway car.

"It looks like the robbers tried to elude capture by taking the back roads," said the inspector. "They lost their way, ran out of gas, and fled on foot."

More police arrived, and the inspector went off to direct a search of the surrounding area.

Haledjian was examining the ground for clues when Carlson finished.

"I've found several prints on the front of the hood and on the gas cap," he said. "They probably belong to the real owner or a gas station attendant. The rest are smudged."

"Too bad," muttered Haledjian. His brows knitted thoughtfully as he watched Carlson open the door of his patrol car and climb in.

Suddenly Haledjian shouted to one of the officers, "Stop that man!"

Why?

Carlson gave himself away by dusting the steering wheel first. A genuine fingerprint expert would have started at the most likely source of clear prints — the front door windows. Carlson confessed: He had subdued the real fingerprint expert assigned to the case and had taken his place in order to destroy the holdup gang's prints.

The Case of the
MODEL
UNIVERSE

"What's it now?" asked Dr. Haledjian. "A uranium mine, sunken bullion, or a pill that converts dishwater into high octane gasoline?"

"Nothing as paltry as that, old chap," answered Bertie Tilford, a young Englishman with more get-rich-quick ideas than fleas on a monkey. "I'm investing in the universe."

Bertie paused to observe the effect of his words. Then he qualified, "Or at least as much of the universe as can be seen by our most powerful telescopes."

Haledjian merely registered skepticism.

"It's the coming thing, the universe," said Bertie. "Five centuries ago man stood on the threshold of vast discoveries. Columbus brought back reports of a new world. Today, man stands on the threshold of thousands of new worlds!"

"You're planning to buy stock," guessed Haledjian. "On Mars or Venus?"

"On this!" exclaimed Bertie. With a regal gesture he produced a tiny ball. It proved a beautifully wrought one-half inch model of the earth.

"Professor Stanford T. Platt is going to build a model of the universe, as accurate as modern science allows. We'll show it in stadiums and indoor arenas like Madison Square Garden. It'll be educational!"

"And costly," muttered Haledjian.

"You've got to spend to make," returned Bertie. "Prof. Platt is trying to raise a million dollars. He'll need to manufacture thousands of stars and planets and moons and what not. But it'll be a sensation. Every school child in America will want to see this exhibit. Every man and woman! I'm going to buy fifty shares at a hundred dollars apiece."

"And lose every penny of it," said Haledjian. *What was wrong with the scheme?*

Prof. Platt couldn't squeeze his exhibition into the Yankee stadium.

To reproduce even part of the universe in a model scaled down to a half-inch earth would mean that the nearest fixed star must be placed more than 20,000 miles away.

The Case of the
MUGGED
SECRETARY

The body of Shirley Tanner, secretary to an airline president, was found in the alley behind the Wright Printers.

Police theorized that she was the victim of a mugger, who, growing desperate at her struggles, strangled her. Her pocketbook, emptied of cash, was discovered in a garbage pail at the end of the alley.

Investigation disclosed that around noon on the day of her death, a typed note had been left on the desk of a co-worker, Julie Biers.

Inspector Winters showed Dr. Haledjian the note. It read:

Julie:
I accidently spilled indelible ink on all the stationary in stock. I feel so badly that I'm going to the Wright Printers to have more printed at once. I'll be back at two.

Shirley

"Somebody could have spilled the ink, typed the note, and got Miss Tanner's fingerprints on the sheet — all after she was killed. Somebody," said Haledjian, "who wanted her death to look like the unfortunate outcome of a mugging."

"Miss Tanner could leave her office without being seen," said the inspector thoughtfully. "And the note was left while the other girls were at lunch. But what grounds have you for suspecting a carefully planned, premeditated murder?"

"The faked clue," snapped Haledjian.

What was the clue?

Had Miss Tanner, the secretary to an airline president, written the note, she never would have made three elementary errors.

"Accidently," was written instead of "accidentally," "badly" instead of "bad," and "stationary" instead of "stationery."

The Case of the
MURDERED
UNCLE

Eric Armbruster had never left New York City in all his 72 years. What enticed him to the Shelby Arms Hotel in Portland, Oregon, and to his death was a mystery.

There was no mystery about what killed him — a .22 slug above the right ear.

Seated in the office of Inspector Winters in New York City, Dr. Haledjian read the report forwarded by the Portland authorities.

According to the report, the hotel elevator operator remembered taking a middle-aged woman to Armbruster's floor on the night of the murder. He did not take her down again. She had departed, apparently, by the fire stairs.

"Armbruster's next of kin is a niece, Gertrude Armbruster. I expect she'll inherit the bulk of his estate," said the inspector. "I'm going out to tell her of her uncle's death. Hate these jobs. Come along, will you?"

At the niece's apartment, the inspector bowed, mumbled a bit, and finally got out his message.

"I'm sorry I must tell you this. Your Uncle Eric was shot to death in a Portland hotel six hours ago."

The niece, a plump woman of 50, collapsed into a chair and covered her face with her hands.

"Do you know why your uncle made the trip?" asked the inspector.

Gertrude Armbruster shook her head. "No, he doesn't know a soul in Oregon. All his business connections and friends are in New York."

Haledjian glanced at the inspector, who by then was getting ready to make the arrest.

Why?

Although she could not have heard of her uncle's slaying, the niece knew he died in Portland, Oregon.

As the state was not told her, she had no way of knowing which of a dozen Portlands was the site of the murder—unless she was involved.

The Case of the
MYSTERIOUS GROCERIES

"A punk who was caught holding up a filling station yesterday has confessed to several unsolved crimes," Inspector Winters told Dr. Haledjian.

"He named Red Kirk as his partner in a supermarket holdup a few years back.

"This morning," went on the inspector, "I picked up a search warrant and visited Kirk's last known address, a boarding house on Waco. Kirk wasn't in, but his roommate, Les Curran, a counterfeiter, showed up at noon. He denied knowing where Kirk was.

"This is the last day of the month. So Kirk, who by the way is a vegetarian, has only to keep moving and stay out of sight for 30 days. In another month the statute of limitations will expire on his supermarket job. He'll be in the clear.

"The part that baffles me is the groceries I found on Kirk's bed," concluded the inspector. I can't figure them. There were six coffee beans, eight boxes of cocoa, 10 tomatoes, four pieces of toast, 14 boxes of hominy, 21 tea bags, and 27 cubes of sugar!"

After a moment's reflection, Haledjian said:

"Kirk plans to keep moving about the country next month to avoid capture, but you should have no trouble apprehending him. The nearest place to find him is —"

Where?

Toast, N.C.

Haledjian deduced that the foodstuffs were an itinerary in code for Kirk's roommate, Curran, with the number of each article standing for the day of the month in which Kirk would be at a particular place.

Hence Kirk's itinerary was: Toast, N.C.; Coffee, Ga.; Cocoa, Fla.; Tomato, Miss.; Hominy, Okla.; Tea, S.D.; Sugar, Idaho.

The Case of the
OLYMPIC
ATHLETE

"I've locked the gates," said the aged caretaker. "Nobody will be able to get in or out of the grounds tonight, Doctor."

Dr. Haledjian nodded approvingly and returned to the mansion of Mildred Emerson. The young heiress had asked him to her house party as a combination guest and protector. In the past week she had received several telephone calls threatening her life.

The most conspicuous of the house guests was the unsteady figure of Biff Walters. The Olympic pole vaulter was rapidly drinking his way out of Mildred's affections.

At midnight, as Haledjian was undressing, he heard Mildred scream, and then the reports of two quick shots. Throwing on a robe, he rushed to her bedroom.

"The jewels — stolen!" she gasped. "The thief tried to kill me!"

"Did you see who it was?" demanded Haledjian.

"No—I didn't see anyone. It all occurred so swiftly. I fainted, and when I came to, my jewel box was gone."

"Was your door locked?"

"Yes. I had to unlock it to admit you," the trembling girl replied. "The thief must have climbed through the window."

"Impossible," said Haledjian, drawing back the curtains. "It's a sheer 15-foot drop to the ground."

Below, Haledjian saw the caretaker playing his flashlight in the flowerbed beneath the window.

"See any ladder marks?" inquired the criminologist.

"Nope. Just a bunch of footprints and a single hole about as big as my wrist and a couple inches deep," was the reply.

"I might have guessed you'd find exactly that," said Haledjian.

Whom did he suspect?

Mildred Emerson — of trying to frame Biff Walters, of whom she was tiring. The imprints in the flowerbed were supposed to indicate Biff had used a pole to climb to her window.

Although the girl had claimed she did not see the thief, she had screamed before the shots were fired.

The Case of the
PETITE WIFE

"I'll have to take you down to headquarters, Mr. Logan," said Inspector Winters. "Your car was identified as the one seen speeding away from the corner of Everett and Rose, where the Burton boy was hit this morning."

"Obviously, there's been a mistake," said Logan, a huge man of six feet six inches. "I haven't driven the car in two days."

"Larry Appleson, a playmate of the injured boy, is pretty sure it was your car, and driven by a big man," replied the inspector.

Logan laughed genially. "Now I know there's been an error. The only person who drove the car this morning was my wife. She hardly can be mistaken for a man."

The inspector glanced at Mrs. Logan, a pale blonde, hardly five feet tall.

"I put it to you, inspector," said Logan. "Could you mistake Claire for a man?"

"No," agreed the inspector. "One other

thing. The hit-run car made a lot of noise, as if it had muffler trouble."

"Listen for yourself," invited Logan, leading the inspector to the garage.

Taking a set of keys from his pocket, he slipped comfortably behind the wheel, and started the motor without delay. He backed the car onto the street and drove twice around the block.

"The car operated noiselessly," the inspector told Haledjian later. "But even before I discovered it had a new muffler, I knew Logan was lying."

Haledjian knew too. Did you?

Although Logan claimed his five-foot wife was the only person to drive the car that morning, he was able to slip "comfortably behind the wheel."

Since he was six and a half feet tall, he would have had to adjust the seat from her position to his if she had really been the last driver.

The Case of the
PHONY FIGHT

"A woman's mind is the one insoluble mystery," admitted Dr. Haledjian to the thin, bespectacled youth. "But I'll help you if I can."

Cyril Makin nodded gratefully, cleared his throat, and said, "I'd been secretly in love with Gladys Brewster for two years. My chances seemed hopeless. She's one of those big outdoorsy girls, a champion skier and swimmer. I never did better than assistant manager of the high school basketball team. Can't see twenty feet without my glasses.

"I knew she'd never take me seriously unless I proved myself a man. So I enlisted the aid of Rocky Armstrong, the heavyweight boxing champion.

"He had staged private 'fights' before, I was relieved to learn. Even had a straight fee for getting knocked down. Two thousand dollars, in advance. A lot of money, but I paid.

"The next night I escorted Gladys to Rocky's

Steak House on 12th street. The place was crowded as usual, and we were asked to wait in a small anteroom by ourselves.

"Presently Rocky entered, eyed Gladys up and down, and made an improper remark. I demanded a retraction. He laughed at me.

'I don't like to do this,' I said and, slipping my glasses into my breast pocket, threw up my fists and went for him.

"Gladys screamed. Rocky waded in, pounded me unmercifully about the body. I pressed on, undaunted. A smart left to the jaw laid him down and out, just as we'd rehearsed it.

"'Let's get out of here,' I snapped, replacing my glasses and grabbing Gladys. She looked at me mutely, sheer worship shining in her eyes.

"It was in the taxicab that the looked changed. 'You staged the fight!' she cried. 'You phony!'

"I've called her countless times since, but she won't speak with me. How the dickens did she know the fight was faked?"

Haledjian knew. Do you?

fight — unbroken.

Gladys knew the champ had pulled his punches; although he had pounded Cyril "un-mercifully about the body," Cyril had removed his eyeglasses from his breast pocket after the

The Case of the
PIRATED
YACHT

On a clear summer night five armed men in a power skiff chugged alongside the yacht, *Coral Reef*.

Too big to be tied up at the Wilson Yacht Club piers, the yacht lay at anchorage in deeper waters. The five armed men boarded her, put the captain and his crew of three into the skiff, and headed the *Coral Reef* out to sea.

No word of her was had for a month.

"The night she was pirated," Inspector Winters told Dr. Haledjian, "the *Coral Reef* carried a cargo destined for Italy — medicines worth millions."

"I never believed the story the captain and his crew told about being surprised," said Haledjian. "I take it you have news?"

"This morning I received a telegram from a Federal agent," said the inspector. "He reports the *Coral Reef* is at Anchorage, Alaska, abandoned and empty."

The telephone on the inspector's desk rang.

"That must be the captain of the *Coral Reef*. I placed a call to him in Chicago," said the inspector.

He picked up the receiver and spoke. "Captain Shea? I have good news. The *Coral Reef* is at Anchorage. You will? Fine."

Hanging up, the inspector said, "The captain said he'll notify the owners at once. Then he'll fly to Alaska and take possession of the yacht if he is able to."

"But he won't be able to," said Haledjian, grinning. "You'll have him under arrest for piracy within the hour!"

Why?

Over the telephone the inspector had simply said the yacht was "at Anchorage."

Had the captain truly been an innocent victim of the piracy, he should have heard "at anchorage," and asked, "Where?"

Instead, he knew immediately she was at the port, Anchorage, in Alaska.

The Case of the
POISONED
MICE

A bright glitter of reminiscence came to Dr. Haledjian's eye when Octavia, his fair dinner companion, ordered a cheese and celery souffle.

"I am reminded of a mice poisoning case in England many years ago," he said.

"Mice?" squeaked Octavia. "Don't tell me! You'll ruin my appetite!"

Haledjian ignored the protest.

"I had gone to visit the Mousery of Freddie Monte-Culver outside London," began the sleuth. "It was a time when mouse shows were the craze. A prize mouse was not only colored black and white, but blue, red, chocolate, lilac, and even champagne.

"Freddie wasn't in, but Reeves, his assistant, a genial fellow in a tight-fitting white lab coat, showed me around.

"'A perfect mouse should have a tail the same length as the body,' he explained, slipping a stud mouse a bit of cheese. 'A superbly or uniquely colored specimen can be sold for as much as $750.'

"The next day I telephoned Freddie as I was departing for the Continent. I learned to my dismay — but hardly to my surprise—that many of his best mice had died mysteriously.

" 'Fire your assistant,' " I advised.

How come?

Haledjian knew that Reeves was feeding the mice cheese, which poisoned them.

A thousand mice and more can be fed oats, milk, bread, and raw eggs inexpensively and safely — but never cheese. Cheese overheats their blood!

The Case of the
POWER
FAILURE

Turner opened the refrigerator in his mountain cabin and withdrew an ice tray. By the candlelight, Dr. Haledjian could see his hands were trembling as he deposited three cubes into a highball glass.

Haledjian could hardly blame the young novelist for trembling. They had just come from the den, where Turner's housekeeper, Lucy, lay dead of a broken neck.

"I thought she was a burglar," exclaimed Turner, downing his drink.

"After the generator failed four days ago," he continued, "I lost all electrical power up here. I'd rented the cabin to be alone in order to put a high polish on my latest novel. I like to work at night, but not without lights. So I moved to a motel in town.

"Two hours ago — a little after midnight — I came back here to get some notes. I'd put down my flashlight to unlock a desk drawer when Lucy jumped me from behind. I guess she thought I was a burglar.

"She's trained in judo, and in the dark I thought I was being attacked by a man. I hit her — and you saw what happened. She fell against the fireplace and broke her neck.

"I heard you were in town, and I fetched you immediately," concluded Turner.

"Why?" demanded Haledjian. "You knew your housekeeper was dead. And if you brought me up here for the purpose of testing your story, I suggest you improve it before the police question you!"

How come?

Turner claimed that he had been without electrical power for "four days," and in the darkness he mistook his housekeeper for a burglar. However, had he really been without power for four days, the ice cubes in the refrigerator would have turned to water!

The Case of the
PROVOKED
ASSAULT

"You put Everet Evans in the hospital with a broken jaw, but he isn't going to charge you with assault," said Dr. Haledjian. "Mind telling me what this is all about?"

"Evans," answered John Wilmot, "is a gambler and a scoundrel. I've forbidden my son Cliff to associate with him, though Cliff worships the blackguard.

"Three days ago Cliff went to Calred City to visit an aunt for the day, and yesterday I received an anonymous telephone call.

"The caller swore that Cliff had gone with Evans to his hunting lodge, which is five miles from Calred City.

"An hour after the call, I had lunch with Evans and innocently asked him to have me up to the lodge for a weekend of hunting. He was reluctant, said the lodge hadn't been used for months, but he finally consented.

"Upon reaching the lodge, we immediately

went out to hunt. We shot two rabbits, and while Evans prepared the game, I looked around.

"It's hard to tell whether a place has been occupied recently, especially if care is taken to cover up. Evans observed my guarded snooping with a supercilious air.

"The lodge was well provisioned with food and drink. We ate the rabbits and some canned fruit. I was just taking a swallow of sweet cider from a half-filled jug — Evans drank Irish whiskey — when he said:

" 'I know what you're really hunting for up here, John.'

"That's when I hit him and broke his jaw," concluded Wilmot.

"I don't condone violence," said Haledjian. "Still, I can readily understand why Evans isn't taking you to court."

Why not?

Evans lied when he said "the lodge hasn't been used for months," since John Wilmot drank "sweet cider from a half-filled jug." Had the cider been standing in the jug for months, it would have fermented and tasted sour.

The Case of the
PURSE
SNATCHER

Dr. Haledjian was in Inspector Winter's office when Bumbles Brasoon, the nation's most inexpert petty crook, was brought in for questioning.

"The charge is purse snatching outside the new theater on Washington Avenue," snapped the inspector.

"It's a case of mistaken identity!" wailed Bumbles.

"The complainant, Mrs. Ruth Fogerty, didn't give you her pocketbook now, did she?" chided the inspector.

"No, but the real crook did," said Bumbles. "I'll tell you what happened, and it's the truth. I swear on my wife's honor!"

"I was walking past the theater thinking about looking for a job when the weather improves. Suddenly I hear a woman scream. This big kid with long hair comes hot-footing past me, carrying a pocketbook.

"He ducks into the alley behind the theater. I give chase like a good citizen. He gets to the theater's fire exit door when he spots me.

"He knows I've got him. So he chucks me the pocketbook, pushes open the door, and slips inside. I'm holding the pocketbook when this rhino of a dame comes charging up the alley with a cop," concluded Bumbles. "I'm innocent!"

After Bumbles had been ushered out, the inspector said to Haledjian, "Mrs. Fogerty isn't certain who snatched her pocketbook. Bumble's story is weak, but it might be true."

"His story is impossible," said Haledjian.

Why?

The "kid" would have had to enter the theater by pulling open the fire exit door, not by pushing it, as Bumbles claimed. Theater fire exit doors open out into the street.

The Case of the
RACETRACK MURDER

The blonde stumbled from the stall shouting, "Please, somebody, in there!"

Dr. Haledjian, who was watching the horses in their early morning workouts, hurried into the stall from which the excited girl had dashed.

Beside a large bay mare, a man attired in horseman's garb lay face down in the straw. An ice pick jutted from a large irregular blood stain on his lower back.

"Dead about eight hours," muttered Haledjian. "That puts the time of the murder about midnight. Pardon me, isn't that blood on the back of your sleeve, miss?"

The blonde pulled the sleeve of her stylish riding habit around and peered at a long smear of blood on the underside.

"Oh," she gasped faintly. "I must have brushed against the wound when I stooped over him just before."

When the police arrived, she said, "I'm Gale Devore. Th-that's Pete Murphy, who trains my mare, Black Bay."

Haledjian asked, "Do you know anyone who had reason to kill Murphy?"

"No," the girl answered. "Except, perhaps . . . Bob Ford. Pete owed him a great deal of money. . . ."

"Fifteen thousand dollars, to be exact," the inspector told Haledjian the next morning. "But Ford, who runs a fish store, swears he hasn't been near Miss Devore's stable for two days. Incidentally, the blood on her sleeve is the same type as the dead man's."

"You made an arrest, I take it?" said Haledjian.

"The suspect is in jail right now," replied the inspector.

Who is the suspect?

Gale Devore, who lied in claiming she got the blood on her sleeve when she "brushed against the wound when I stooped over him just before." As Murphy was dead eight hours by then, his blood would have been too dry to smear her sleeve.

The Case of the
RAILROAD ROBBERY

"What time will we arrive in San Francisco?" asked Dr. Haledjian, as the conductor passed his seat in the Pullman.

"In exactly one hour — at twenty minutes after three," was the reply. "Your first trip to California?"

"No, but my first time to the northern part of the state," replied the famed sleuth.

"Well, you'll like 'Frisco," said the conductor genially. "Great town. Been living there myself for thirty-two — "

Just then a blond young man charged down the aisle shouting, "In compartment 6! Come at once!"

With the blond leading, the conductor and Haledjian rushed to the car directly behind them. A white-haired man was slumped in the seat of compartment 6. He had been knocked unconscious.

"It's Harry Winslow, the New York jeweler,"

said Haledjian. "He's a bit of a showman —
sometimes carries a million dollars in jewels
with him and makes no secret of it."

"Looks like you've hit the motive," said the
conductor, stooping. He picked an empty jewel
case from the floor.

Then he turned sharply to the blond young
man. "Who are you and what were you doing
in this compartment?"

"My name is Clarence Swezy. My compartment is right next door," answered the young
man. "I met Mr. Winslow in the dining car and
he invited me in for a drink before we arrived
in San Francisco."

The jeweler opened his eyes and put his
hand to the bump on the back of his head.
"W-what — who hit me?" he groaned.

"He did," snapped Haledjian, and with a
deft judo hold he rendered powerless the man
he suspected of the jewelry theft.

Which man?

never as " 'Frisco."

refer to the city by its full name, and never,
Second, a resident of San Francisco would
ty," in giving the time.
"twenty minutes after three," but "three-twen-
First, no railroad man would have said
of being an imposter for two reasons.
The conductor, whom Haledjian suspected

82

The Case of the
REVERSED FAUCETS

Dr. Haledjian was strolling past the small house of Thomas Fremont when the back door swung open violently.

A tall man rushed out. "Dr. Haledjian!" he cried. "Come inside! Something dreadful has happened!"

Haledjian recognized Fremont's prodigal nephew Scott. Hastening inside, he found Fremont lying in the living room on his right side, beyond help. His right hand, covered with blood, fumbled at the handle of the knife protruding from his stomach.

"W-water," Fremont gasped.

Scott seemed rooted to the spot. Haledjian dashed into the kitchen, where he encountered difficulty with the faucets. When at last he filled a glass, Fremont was dead.

"Strange that your uncle asked for water," Haledjian said to Scott after the police arrived. "Another thing. The hot and cold faucets in the kitchen are reversed. I turned on the right hand one and immediately got a jet of hot water. The cold water faucet is on the left."

"Uncle was left-handed," explained Scott. "He had all the faucets in the house reversed. He was a bit of an eccentric — lived here alone for years."

"Had you been inside long before you encountered me?"

"No — I had just arrived. I found him stabbed and ran for help."

"Or tried to escape," snapped Haledjian.

Why did Haledjian doubt Scott?

Fremont's gasp for water was intended to lead Haledjian to his murderer — Scott.

It takes a few moments for hot water to come through the pipes, and the fact that one faucet "immediately" gave "a jet of hot water" proved it had been used very recently.

Scott confessed. He had washed the blood from his hands before running from the house.

The Case of the
SCREAMING CAT

"One of your neighbors reported hearing a scream from this house about ten minutes ago," Inspector Winter said. "I'm sorry to intrude, but we happened to be driving nearby, and I thought I'd check on the report myself."

James McNalty stood scowling in the doorway — till he saw the inspector's badge. "There's some mistake," he protested. "B-but come in."

The inspector and Dr. Haledjian left the rain, which had been falling for three hours, and entered the bright and cheerful little house.

"I'll bet Mrs. Hatfield reported the scream," said McNalty. "She lives next door with her cats. I found a gray one camped at my door when I came home ten minutes ago.

"I was tired and wet and impatient," continued McNalty. "The cat didn't move, so I kicked it — harder than I intended. It let out a yowl. A yowl, inspector. Not a scream."

"Is that your station wagon in the back?" inquired Haledjian.

"Yes. I've been away selling for two weeks," said McNalty.

Haledjian peered through the window at the station wagon a moment and suddenly went outside.

"Here, pussy," he murmured gently at the gray cat cowering under the station wagon. He moved one hand along the dry gravel beneath the car and then with a lightning motion seized the cat. Carrying it back into the house, he asked McNalty, "Do you live here alone?"

"With my wife, Mae," was the nervous reply.

"For your sake, I hope she's well," said Haledjian. "If there was a scream, I don't think the cat made it!"

What aroused Haledjian's suspicion?

Had McNalty really come home "ten minutes ago," the gravel under his car would have been wet. Instead it was dry, proving the car had been there before the rain started "three hours" before.

Haledjian believed McNalty had spied the cat under the car and used it as an alibi for the scream.

The Case of the
SECOND WILL

"Young Mark Rall insists he found this in an Old Testament in his uncle's library," said Evans, the attorney. He handed Dr. Haledjian a document as both men sat in the criminologist's study.

Haledjian released a low whistle. The document was a last will and testament. It bequeathed the bulk of Arthur Marx Colby's millions to his 22-year-old nephew, Mark Rall.

"This will is either genuine or a dashedly clever forgery," opined Haledjian. "When did Colby die?"

"Last April — April 21, to be exact," answered Evans. "If this will is genuine, it will mean Colby's two elderly sisters, my clients, will be out a fortune."

"I assume this new will is dated after the one leaving the fortune to your clients?"

"Yes, twelve days later," said Evans.

"When did young Rall find it?"

"Last week," said Evans. "He says he had opened a copy of the Old Testament and there between pages 157 and 158 was this will."

"He's pretty sure of himself," muttered Haledjian.

"He takes pride in a punctilious mind, the young scoundrel," returned Evans. "He's willing to settle out of court — for half his uncle's estate! But I must give him an answer within two hours. Can you spot anything wrong with the will he claims to have found?"

"I'm no expert in the field," concluded the sleuth. "Nevertheless, I should tell young Rall to put this will back where he found it!"

How come?

Rall could not have found the will between pages 157 and 158 as he claimed. Try putting a piece of paper between those pages in the book nearest you!

The Case of the
SILK MANTLE

Police established the following facts:

1. On a beastly hot day, a masked man had entered the Carton's apartment. In attempting to beat from Mrs. Carton the hiding place of her diamond necklace, he had accidentally killed her. He had ransacked the apartment and had fled empty-handed.

2. Mr. Carton, an invalid who had been under sedation during the crime, discovered the body and notified police.

3. Suspicion fell upon Bill, the doorman and an ex-con, who had not reported to work since the slaying.

4. The necklace was safely hidden in the false bottom of a jewelry box in the guest closet near the fireplace. The box rested on the closet shelf above the spot where Mrs. Carton habitually hung her gold silk mantle. She wore this garment in the apartment on chilly days, but never outside the apartment.

Upon ascertaining these facts, Dr. Haledjian asked to be left alone in the apartment with the doorman.

After hearing Bill insist he had never set foot in the apartment, Haledjian shifted a cigarette container and two statuettes on the shelf above the fireplace and rested his elbow there.

"The necklace was right here in the false bottom of a box above the mantle. See for yourself," urged the sleuth. "Come on!"

In a moment, Bill had found the jade box above Mrs. Carton's silk mantle.

After he was clapped under arrest, Haledjian told Inspector Winters, "A criminal should never return to the scene of his crime."

What was Bill's mistake?

Bill insisted he "had never set foot in the apartment," before, yet he knew about the silk mantle in the closet.

An innocent man would have assumed that the necklace was hidden in the cigarette box on the fireplace shelf, or "mantel."

The Case of the
SLEEPING
DEER

When Dr. Haledjian reached the scene of the fatal hunting accident, he found Sheriff Monahan already there.

"The dead man is H. Harvey Morton," said the sheriff. "He and his law partner, Bill Johnson, had been afield two hours when the tragedy struck. Johnson states he missed a shot at a buck, and the bullet pierced Morton's left temple."

Haledjian stooped by the body, which lay face downward, about ten feet from a low thicket. One hand still clutched a rifle. The wound, though messy, was clearly visible, as Morton was hatless.

"I guess I was overanxious," Johnson said remorsefully. "Harvey and I hunted together last year, and we bagged our limit by the second day. But we'd gone four days without a shot before we spotted this big buck.

"He was lying asleep in that little thicket,"

continued Johnson. "It was Harvey's turn — we always agree on who shoots first. I sneaked in closer, believing Harvey was right behind me. But he must have crept in on the far side of the thicket.

"Well, the buck sensed us, because he suddenly rose to his forelegs. Then his rump came up, and Harvey still didn't fire. The buck was ready to bolt, and I knew I'd have to shoot first or lose the big fellow. I missed — and hit poor Harvey."

"Didn't Harvey wear a red hunting cap?" asked Haledjian.

Johnson looked surprised. "Yes . . . He must have lost it in the woods someplace."

Thanking the distraught hunter, Haledjian returned to the sheriff. "I'd check into the firm of Morton and Johnson," he advised. "I've a strong suspicion Johnson had good reason to kill his partner."

Why did Haledjian suspect Johnson?

Johnson's story was clearly an invention. He said the buck rose first on his forelegs. Unfortunately for him, a deer gets off the ground hind-end first.

The Case of the
SLIP OF PAPER

The night clerk in the Jade Motel was the lone witness to the telephone booth slaying of gambler Ken Cobham.

He told police that Cobham had just spun the dial two or three times when a masked gunman shot Cobham twice in cold blood. The killer escaped as Cobham staggered around a corner and fell dead.

"It's a professional job. No clues. Tomorrow I ought to get a visit from Nick the Nose," sighed Inspector Winters.

Sure enough, the following day as the inspector and Dr. Haledjian, the famed criminologist, were going out to lunch, Nick presented himself at headquarters.

"I got a lead on the Cobham murder," the greasy little informer said.

"You haven't had a lead since you won the sack race in second grade," snapped the inspector.

Unruffled by such heartless truth, Nick handed the inspector a torn slip of paper on which was written "Ze-2-"

"You remember Cobham staggered out of the telephone booth?" asked Nick. "He turned a corner and the night clerk lost sight of him for a few seconds?"

"Yeah, the newspapers had that," said the inspector.

"Cobham bumped into Icky Francisco," said Nick. "Cobham dropped a piece of paper. Icky picked it up. The numbers on that paper are part of a telephone number Cobham must have been calling when he was shot. I got the other half of the paper — with the last four numbers — in my pocket. I figure it's worth something big!"

"How's a size 12?" roared the inspector, and planted his foot persuasively on the seat of Nick's pants.

Why did Nick get the boot?

Cobham, who had "just spun the dial two or three times" when he was shot, could not have been dialing a "Ze" number because there is no Z on the dial.
Z is a mobile exchange number, and to be connected the caller must dial operator.

The Case of the
SPEEDING TRAIN

The fat man lay by the railroad embankment, his twisted limbs testifying to the imprudence of leaving a train as it raced at 100 miles per hour.

"Broken neck — probably died instantly," said Dr. Haledjian after a summary examination. "Who is he?"

"Tommy Harner, the New York racketeer," replied Sheriff Monahan. "He must have jumped from the Rocket. It leaves New York for Los Angeles on Tuesday night and passes through here around four Wednesday afternoon. It's the only train by, today."

"What makes you sure Harner jumped?" asked Haledjian.

"For one thing the money in his wallet. For another, his valises."

"Valises?"

"I'll show you," said the sheriff, shading his eyes as he led the way down the tracks toward the setting sun.

After some five hundred yards, the two men came to the first valise. It contained expensive clothes monogrammed TH.

Another two hundred yards farther along lay the second valise. It contained fifty thousand dollars in new twenty dollar bills.

"Counterfeit," said the sheriff. "Apparently someone wanted it, and Harner decided to jump rather than give it up."

"At least that's what someone wants the authorities to believe," said Haledjian. "The killer went to a lot of trouble, but the autopsy will show Harner was slain and then thrown from the train."

How did Haledjian know?

The two valises were found far to the west of the body ("toward the setting sun"), in the same direction as the train traveled (New York to Los Angeles).

Hence, Harner had left the speeding train first and his bags had followed him several seconds later.

The Case of the
SPILLED
BRANDY

In pouring Dr. Haledjian's 20-year-old brandy, Inspector Winters inadvertently spilled a liberal quantity on the carpet. He apologized and chuckled reminiscently. "Last year I arrested a man after he'd spilled some brandy — and not nearly such good stuff as this, either."

"So?" said Haledjian inquiringly.

"I was driving upstate for the weekend," recalled the inspector. "Somehow, I took a wrong turn. I pulled up to a big farmhouse to ask directions.

"As I stopped my car behind a black convertible in the driveway, a young man burst out of the house.

" 'Do you live here?' he shouted excitedly.

"I told him I didn't. Nonetheless he seemed awfully glad to have somebody else around. He said he was a stranger who'd stopped to ask directions a minute before I arrived.

" 'The house is empty — except for a woman

lying on the sofa. I th-think she's dead!' he ex-claimed.

"The woman wasn't dead, but she wasn't very alive. Not with her head bloody and bruises on her throat. I told the excited young man to find some brandy, and he disappeared into the kitchen while I telephoned the police.

"When the young man came back I tried to tell him the brandy was to steady his nerves. But he acted too swiftly. He put the bottle to the unconscious woman's lips. He'd spilled most of it over her chin and throat before I yanked the bottle away.

" 'Leave her alone!' I ordered. And just to make it emphatic, I held my gun on him till the local police could place him under arrest. Luckily, the girl survived. But if I hadn't driven up unexpectedly, he'd have finished choking her to death."

How did the inspector know?

The young man claimed to be a stranger in the big farmhouse. Yet he knew the brandy was kept in the kitchen.

The Case of the
STOLEN BIBLE

Dr. Haledjian put the telephone receiver to his ear and heard the frantic voice of Ted Petrie, a rare-book collector.

"A thief took the hinges off the door of one of my book cabinets and made off with a 16th-century Bible," explained Petrie. "Can you come right over to my place?"

Half an hour later, Haledjian stood on the second floor of Petrie's home and examined the small, empty book cabinet. The glass door, unhinged, lay on the carpet.

"I was downstairs watching television," said Petrie. "I went to the kitchen for a bite to eat and suddenly a man dashed down the stairs and out the front door. He was carrying the Bible.

"Of course I chased him. At the corner of Vine and Davis, I lost him in the crowd watching the St. Patrick's Day parade. I stopped at the first pay telephone and called you.

"I always keep the cabinet locked. I expect

the noise of the television kept me from hearing the thief at work upstairs."

"The Bible is insured?" asked Haledjian.

"Yes, for a fortune," answered Petrie. "But money can't replace such a book!"

"Then I suggest you put it back," said Haledjian. "I don't believe a word of your story!"

Why not?

At the time he telephoned Haledjian, Petrie had no way of knowing exactly how the cabinet on the second floor had been opened.

The Case of the
STOLEN
PAINTING

Dr. Haledjian arrived ten minutes early for his dinner appointment with Arthur Corning. The evening was to be a celebration. Arthur had just been bequeathed a brownstone house by his cousin, Harriet Trease.

The youth was far from the prototype of the happy heir as he greeted Haledjian.

"Good heavens, if you'd only got here five minutes sooner!" he exclaimed. "The paintings. They've been stolen!"

"Calm yourself and tell me what happened," said Haledjian.

"As you know, my cousin had assembled a modest art collection," said the young man. "Her six favorite oils hung in her study — two by Picasso, two by Renoir, and one each by Turner and Constable. The second-rate works of first-rate artists.

"Ten minutes ago I was alone in the study," went on the youth. "The burglar came up be-

101

hind me, announced he had a gun, and ordered me to face the wall by the Renoir.

"He took down the five pictures and told me to hand him the Renoir. Then he slipped out."

"Without your seeing his face," said Haledjian skeptically.

"Wrong," Arthur snapped. "I saw him in the reflection of the glass over the Renoir. I can identify him, and I shall!"

"The pictures were insured?"

"Yes. I don't stand to lose anything, luckily."

"You mean you stand to pocket a tidy sum and still keep the paintings," said Haledjian. "You invited me here to test your story before applying for the insurance, didn't you?"

What was the flaw in Arthur's story?

Arthur lied when he said he saw the burglar's face "in the reflection of the glass over the Renoir." All the stolen paintings were oils, and oils are never framed under glass.

The Case of the
TARDY
WITNESS

"The fight happened last May 30th, and it's just now coming up on the court calendar," said Kronke, the attorney for young Arthur Monroe. "Frankly, I didn't give my client much of a chance. A neighbor who saw the whole thing said Arthur struck Mr. Gilman first."

"What's changed your attitude suddenly?" asked Dr. Haledjian.

"A new witness, John Craft, turned up yesterday. He's a close buddy of Arthur's and claims to have seen the fight from the bank directly across the street. His version is that Mr. Gilman hit Arthur first. I want you to check his story before I put him on the stand."

Haledjian consented. John Craft was ushered in and related what he had seen.

"I'd gone into the First National Bank to make a deposit, but it was lunchtime, and there were long lines in front of all the clerks. I didn't feel like waiting, so I left.

"As I got to the door I had a perfect view of Arthur and Old Man Gilman approaching each other on the opposite sidewalk. Arthur told me how Old Man Gilman was always needling him. He said if Gilman ever started something, why he'd just walk away.

"Old Man Gilman wouldn't let him walk away. He blocked Arthur and punched him twice in the jaw. Arthur reached up to ward off another blow. Old Man Gilman tripped and hit his neck against Arthur's raised hand.

"That's when the neighbor looked out. She saw Old Man Gilman stagger and fall to the pavement on his face. I guess he got the brain concussion from falling so hard."

"Why didn't you speak up at the time, instead of letting months pass?" asked Haledjian.

"I — I didn't want to get involved," stammered Craft. "I've done time in a reformatory."

"And you'll do more time for perjury if you ever repeat that story under oath," said Haledjian harshly.

What was Craft's lie?

Craft could not have been emerging from the bank opposite the scene of the fight. The fight occurred on May 30th, Decoration Day, when all banks are closed.

The Case of the
THEFT AT THE CIRCUS

Willie the clown, still attired in his comic knight suit of pots and pans, clanked and clattered to a pile of folded chairs and sat down disconsolately.

"It's true I passed Princess Minerva's trailer five minutes ago. But I didn't steal her money!"

"I saw him slip out of the trailer," insisted Kathy Winslow, an aerial ballerina. "He looked around, stuck a bag under his arm, and hurried off. I couldn't mistake him in that get-up!"

"Come, now, Kathy. You're overwrought," said Princess Minerva, the circus' trapeze star. "Everyone knows where I keep my cash. Why would Willie rob me? We've been together with the circus for twenty years!"

"Calm down yourself," cautioned Dr. Haledjian as he finished bandaging Princess Minerva's head. "You're going to be out of action a couple of days."

"Never mind me," said Princess. "Find the

thief. I was sitting with my back to the door reading. I never heard the louse sneak in. What did he hit me with?"

"This," answered Haledjian, holding up a battered pot.

"It's not mine!" protested the clown.

"Don't believe him," said Kathy.

Haledjian studied Willie. His eyes narrowed.

"Your attempt to frame Willie is contemptible," he said to Kathy.

How did Haledjian know?

Princess Minerva said she had not heard the thief enter her trailer. That ruled out Willie in his clanking and clattering knight's rig.

When confronted with this inconsistency, Kathy confessed to the robbery.

The Case of the
13 ROSES

The single window and door to Wayne Hector's rented room were both locked from the inside. Police officers, acting on a tip, broke in and found the 40-year-old librarian on the bed, dead of a gunshot wound.

"The flower vendor at the 103rd Street subway station called us this morning," Inspector Winters told Dr. Haledjian over the telephone.

"You see, every Friday evening for ten years Hector bought 13 coral roses. Yesterday he missed his regular stop, and the vendor became worried.

"The way it looks," went on the inspector, "Hector locked the door and window and shot himself while sitting on the bed. He fell over on his right side, dropping the pistol to the carpet. The door key was in his vest pocket."

"What about the roses he bought the previous week?"

"They were wilted and dead in a vase of water on the windowsill," said the inspector. "Hector died about five days ago."

"Does the carpet cover the entire floor?"

"Yes, to about an inch of the walls," replied the inspector.

"Are there any blood stains on the floor, windowsill, or carpet?"

"No, nothing except a little dust. Only on the bed are there bloodstains."

"In that case," said Haledjian, "you had better request laboratory tests of the carpet for bloodstains," said Haledjian. "Somebody with a key to Hector's room killed him as he stood by the window. Then the murderer cleaned up where Hector fell and arranged the body on the bed to make death look like suicide."

How did Haledjian know?

The dead roses on the window sill, after two weeks in the room, should have cast petals on the carpet. Yet the area around the flowers showed "nothing except a little dust."

Haledjian deduced that the petals had been thoughtlessly picked up by the murderer cleaning up the blood.

The Case of the
THREE
CUCUMBERS

Dr. Haledjian stopped at the street peddler's vegetable stand on the corner of Worth and Station streets.

"Three cucumbers, please," he said. "Nice ones."

The youthful peddler selected three cucumbers and dropped them into a brown paper bag.

"Three nice ripe ones, mister," he said, handing the famous sleuth the bag and his change.

Opening the bag, Haledjian checked the three green, rough-skinned vegetables, and bumped into a heavy woman carrying a shoulder-strap pocketbook.

He had barely muttered his apologies when a black car turned the corner. It moved slowly toward the entrance of the National Trust Company bank on the opposite side of the street.

Haledjian glanced quickly up and down the block. Besides the heavy woman and the fruit peddler, two other persons were outdoors.

A tall, natty man was adjusting and readjusting his tie in the reflection of a shoe store window. He seemed dissatisfied with his improvements and repeated them over and over.

Near the bank door, an elderly woman was nervously turning the pages of a bank deposit book.

Haledjian had no chance to intercept the robbers who, a moment later, dashed from the bank and escaped in the black car.

But he did apprehend the gang's lookout. *Whom did he apprehend?*

The vegetable peddler, an obvious phony, who called the green cucumbers "ripe." Ripe cucumbers are yellow.

The Case of the
TIMELY NEIGH

The radio newscast carried a report of the death of writer Bill Quist near Strandville. According to the report, Quist had swerved his sports car from his lane and crashed head-on with a green sedan driven by R. J. Phelps, who escaped with a broken arm and lacerations. Both cars tumbled off the road after colliding.

Dr. Haledjian quickly put through a telephone call to the Strandville police. "I've known Bill Quist for years," he told the police chief. "I can't believe he was at fault and I'd like a chance to clear his name."

The chief's tone was snappish. "Quist was to blame, and that's certain. The accident occurred on the hairpin turn due west of the Fleetwood Riding Academy. Ted Dennison, the riding master, saw the whole thing."

Despite the chief's resentment of big-city snoopers, Haledjian drove up to Strandville. A half hour of questioning established that not only was the injured man, R. J. Phelps, a local bigwig, but also the brother-in-law of the only eye-witness to the accident, Ted Dennison. Haledjian spoke with Dennison late in the afternoon.

"I saw it plainly," said the riding master. "I was just mounting Nelly Bly — that little chestnut mare there."

"What made you glance toward the road?"

"She did," said Dennison with a smirk. "I'd got one foot in the stirrup when all of a sudden she neighed, turned her head to the left, and looked at the road almost expectantly. Over her back I saw the two cars — that fellow Quist jumped the center line."

"Why weren't any tire marks found on the road?"

"The fact is," answered Dennison. "The rain washed away all the marks."

"The fact is," retorted Haledjian. "You never saw the accident."

What was the basis for Haledjian's accusation?

The mare looked "left" to see the road, which was "due west." Hence she stood with her head to the north. Therefore, Dennison, in witnessing the accident "over her back," would have been mounting on the right side, a fault no riding master ever commits.

The Case of the
TREASURE MAP

"I asked you over to settle an ugly dispute between my two sons," John Boyd told Dr. Haledjian.

"The affair is this. Last month Carl and Eddie rented a luxury sailboat and cruised the Keys. On one of the islands Carl found a piece of cloth with geographic markings.

"It was a map — like Captain Kidd made — on cloth, drawn with dye. The map became soaked and ruined. I want you to hear each boy's story," concluded Boyd.

Eddie, a youth of 20, told his story first.

"We lay becalmed at low tide off Brake Island," he said. "I was in the salon when I noticed a hole in the side no more than six inches above the waterline.

"I plugged the hole with a piece of folded cloth — I didn't realize it was the map! — I found under the desk. I don't know how it got there, I swear. When the tide rose, the map became wet."

Carl, the older brother, told a different story.

"Eddie was sore because I didn't immediately promise to share any treasure with him. I saw him sneak out of the salon and throw something overboard — a balled-up piece of cloth.

"Suspicious, I dived after it. The water was clear and calm as glass. I recovered the cloth immediately — but too late! On board, I saw it was the map, ruined!"

When Boyd was again alone with Haledjian, he said: "I can't verify Eddie's story about a hole near the waterline. The sailboat sank the day after the incident. I simply don't know who is lying!"

Haledjian knew. Do you?

Eddie lied. The sailboat would have risen with the tide, and so the water never would have reached the hole and wet the map.

The Case of the
TWO BANK ROBBERS

Until Dr. Haledjian read the account, there never had been a question of the fate of the two men who robbed the bank at Silver City in '81.

Obviously, they had drowned in the Ki River.

The facts were:

The night before the robbery, Luke Tigert, the banker, brought his horse to Abe Wilson, the blacksmith. Abe was putting new shoes on two horses Luke had never seen before in Silver City, a huge piebald and a stubby bay mare.

Luke overheard Abe tell his helper the surprising fact that both horses wore the same size shoes.

The following afternoon, Abe and his helper robbed the bank. Abe rode off on the piebald, his helper on the little mare.

For several miles the pair kept to the mountains, whose rocky paths retained no hoofprints. Then apparently confused in the gathering darkness, they cut across soft ground to the Ki River.

The two sets of hoofprints, one spaced farther apart than the other, were there for the posse to read in the morning.

The hoofprints led from the rocky path to a yard-wide gap in the bushes which ran along the river for several miles in each direction. A foot beyond the bushes, the ground dropped 200 feet to the water.

"The blacksmith's maneuver cleverly duped the posse," Haledjian told Octavia. "He let them think both riders and horses perished going over the cliff."

What had the blacksmith really done?

The blacksmith had ridden the huge piebald to the gap in the bushes. Then, to imitate the shorter stride of the little mare, he had returned the piebald to the rocky path — going backward.
A horse, like a man, takes shorter steps going backward than forward.

The Case of the
TWO
MRS. BRAUNS

"Konrad Braun, the West German jeweler, died of natural causes last week in his hotel room," said Inspector Winters. "His estate, reputedly over half a million, will go to his bride."

"Bride?" Haledjian raised an eyebrow. "Braun was past seventy, wasn't he?"

"Apparently he married secretly just before sailing for America. He wired his American partner that his bride would join him in New York a week later. Other than that Mrs. Braun was a piano teacher, we don't know anything about her. Today she showed up — or two of them did. Both have all the necessary papers and know everything about Braun. But one is an imposter."

Haledjian consented to accompany the inspector to the home of the murdered man's American partner. In the living room, the two

Mrs. Brauns, a blonde and a brunette, sat glowering at one another. Both were robust, thirty-ish, and pretty.

Haledjian shook hands first with the blonde, and winced. Her grip left a red welt where her ring had bitten into his fingers. The brunette, who looked equally formidable, wore rings on almost every finger. In self protection, Haledjian merely bowed. "Would you play the piano for me?" he requested.

The brunette went smoothly into a Chopin Nocturne, her muscular fingers a-glitter. Haledjian counted three sapphire rings and a wedding band on her left hand, and three diamonds of assorted sizes on her right.

When she finished, the blonde attacked the keyboard, playing the same nocturne as though to outshine her rival. Musically she did as well, though her single plain wedding band left her far behind in the jewelry contest.

When the last note died, Haledjian said, "Suppose you tell us why you are posing as Mrs. Braun!"

To which one did Haledjian speak?

To the bejeweled brunette, who wore her marriage ring on the left hand, the American custom. The blonde wore her band on the right hand (the hand she shook with) after the German tradition.

The Case of the
UNKNOWN
BLONDE

"Pinky Kempton's story about a blonde in a plaid skirt and tight gray sweater is pretty weak," said Inspector Winters. "But unless we break it, we'll never find the gang who tried to hold up the National City Bank yesterday."

"You're convinced Kempton is involved?" asked Haledjian.

"He's been used as a lookout before," replied the inspector. "About the time of the holdup, two police officers noticed him loitering on the corner half a block from the bank.

"The way it figures is this," continued the inspector, "when things suddenly went wrong in the bank, the three masked bandits sprinted for their car. They didn't have time to haul in Kempton, so they left him on the corner.

"We picked him up this morning for questioning. He says he was out walking and had stopped to watch a blonde whom nobody else on the block remembers seeing.

"This mysterious blonde, according to Kempton, was strolling on the opposite side of the street, looking over her left shoulder and primping herself in the reflection of the store windows.

"When she got to the Beford Shoe Store window, she stopped and slowly did an about face. Watching her window image, she adjusted her skirt zipper and smoothened her sweater at the waist. She opened her purse, but noticing Kempton staring at her, hastened down the street.

"As she turned the corner, Kempton says three masked men dashed out of the bank and into a waiting sedan. He didn't get the license plate number, of course."

Haledjian pursed his lips thoughtfully. "Kempton's story has one slight flaw, inspector. Confront him with it, and he may break down."

What was the flaw?

According to Kempton, the blonde was looking over her left shoulder at her reflection, and then "did an about-face" and, still gazing at her reflection, "adjusted her skirt zipper." This meant she zipped her skirt on the right side. Unfortunately for Kempton, women's skirts zip on the left side.

The Case of the
UNKNOWN
BROTHER

Mrs. Sydney, New York's most illustrious party-giver, settled back in her dinner chair. With an eccentric smile, she applied herself to a favorite pastime — trying to confound the deductive prowess of Dr. Haledjian.

"My childhood playmate, Jedediah Wright, ran away from home when he was twelve," she began. "For years he lived by odd jobs. But in 1927 he settled in Michigan and made millions in copper.

"Unfortunately Jed never married. On his deathbed he summoned his faithful housekeeper and handed her a fat envelope containing cash, deeds, and securities.

"His parents had passed away a decade earlier. Jed's only living kin was a brother. 'Give this envelope to my brother, Alf,' the dying man instructed the housekeeper.

"The poor, distracted woman had never seen Alf in her life. Her only clue was a yellowed photograph set in a double frame with one of Jed. Unfortunately, the pictures were taken when both were boys of ten, fifty-five years before.

"Moreover, the only clue to Alf's whereabouts was a letter postmarked the previous month from Los Angeles.

"The housekeeper traveled to Los Angeles and advertised the purpose of her visit. Soon a hundred aged men were camped outside her hotel door.

"Although she had never seen Alf and knew nothing about him, she was able to pick him out of the bevy of imposters!"

"My dear Mrs. Sydney, to what ends will you go to stump an old sleuth?" said Haledjian with a reproachful sigh. "The answer is elementary."

How did the housekeeper know Alf?

Because of her one clue — and yours — the photograph. It was taken "when both boys were ten, fifty-five years ago." Hence, Alf and Jed were twins!

The Case of the
VANISHING HOSTAGE

Mrs. Sydney, the dowager who owned more of Manhattan Island than anyone since the Indians, had satisfied every whim save one. She had never stumped Dr. Haledjian.

So the master sleuth knew the game of outwit-the-detective was on again when Mrs. Sydney set down her after-dinner cordial and regarded him with a triumphant eye.

"A desperate thief," she began, "broke into a Miami Beach motel at 2 A.M. and knocked out the night clerk. The clerk, however, recovered quickly and called the police.

"When they arrived, the detective in charge shouted to the thief to give himself up as the motel was surrounded.

"The thief was in suite 113, occupied by a Detroit family — a grandmother, a mother, and two daughters. He ordered the grandmother to the window and gave the terrified woman a message to relay through the window.

"The grandmother informed the detective that the thief would release three women on the condition that he withdrew his men for half an hour.

"Thinking quickly, the detective shouted back — "

Mrs. Sydney paused, smiling craftily. "Now, doctor, can you tell me what the detective shouted back that permitted all the women — the grandmother, mother, and two daughters — to walk out of the motel unharmed?"

"Really, madame," Haledjian reproached. "I should take offense at such an old word-teaser in new trimmings. The detective shouted — "

What?

The detective shouted back, "Agreed."

The grandmother, mother, and two daughters marched out unharmed, for they numbered only three persons. The mother was both mother and daughter.

The Case of the
WATER NYMPH

Ivers, the insurance adjuster, passed the auction brochure to Dr. Haledjian and tapped a line.

Haledjian read, "Item 37, Water Nymph, undetermined alloy. Weight, 26 pounds. Height, 17½ inches."

"Thomas Covington purchased the statue three weeks ago at this auction in Los Angeles for $20," said Ivers. "He had it added to his personal property policy, placing the value at $10,000. It never arrived at his New York City apartment. He's put in a claim for $10,000!"

"What proof is there that it is lost?"

"The auction manager told me he mailed it to Covington's New York address," replied Ivers. "But, said the manager, he never was advised of its new worth, and so he sent it by ordinary mail — uninsured and unregistered. We can't trace it!"

"Can Covington substantiate its jump in value?"

"The jump is legitimate," replied Ivers. "A Texas oil-man arrived too late to bid on the statue. He telephoned Covington at his Los Angeles hotel, explained the statue was a long-lost heirloom, and offered $10,000 for it.

"Covington agreed to sell the statue when he reached New York. He added it to his insurance but, he says, forgot to notify the auction house about the increased value."

"So your company will have to find the statue or pay the claim," said Haledjian.

The criminologist smiled and added:

"Covington and the auction manager are in cohoots. They plan to collect the insurance money and then sell the statue, getting $20,000 for a $20 investment!"

What made Haledjian so sure?

The auction manager's story of mailing the 26-pound statue to New York City was an obvious lie.

The maximum weight the postal service will carry in first class post offices, like New York City, is 25 pounds.

126

The Case of the
WORLD
TRAVELER

"Moscow Memories," by Nina Virve, had been a runaway best seller for three months when Dr. Haledjian received a telephone call from the book's publisher, Alf Shuller.

"When Mrs. Virve died last month, we held up the royalty payment," said Shuller. "She left no kin, or so we thought. But a husband, who according to the book died in Odessa in 1910, has turned up, claiming the royalties. He'll be in my office at ten. Can you come over?"

Haledjian agreed, and in the publisher's office met Gregori Virve, a distinguished looking gentleman of seventy-odd, suitably equipped with a Russian passport, as well as with birth and marriage certificates.

After an exchange of pleasantries, Haledjian said, "Your wife wrote that you died of pneumonia. Curious you didn't inform her that you survived."

"Curious by American standards only," replied Virve. "You see, the marriage was arranged by our parents. It was short, unhappy.

Six months after the wedding I contracted small pox, not pneumonia. Through a mix-up at the hospital, my death was falsely recorded. I decided against correcting the error."

"My compliments on your English," said Haledjian. "I suppose you prospered and traveled a good bit since your alleged death."

"As Boris Novak I was quite successful in the textile line. Two years after my reported demise, I sold my business to a large Leningrad firm, retaining a share in the profits. Since then I've traveled extensively. When I collect the money from Nina's book, I intend to settle in London permanently. I have no love for my native land under the Communists."

After Virve departed, Alf Shuller said, "Everything appears in order. What do you think, doctor?"

"I'd let Inspector Winters examine his papers. I've a strong feeling they are forgeries."

Why did Haledjian believe the husband an imposter?

The report of Virve's death was issued in 1910, and yet the man claiming to be Virve said he'd sold his business two years later to a "large Leningrad firm" — a slip a real Russian, much less an outspoken anti-Communist, never would have made.

In 1912 Leningrad was still called St. Petersburg.